The C

The Num

Well, you guys wanted more, so here it is, my second collection of jokes, puns and one-liners. If it makes you laugh, job done eh?

Don't forget my Twitter feed @robertwlk for a daily joke or three.

www.robertwilkinsonauthor.com

robertwilkinsonauthot@gmail.com

Oh, and I do novels as well.

Here goes, In no particular order....

- "Where did all these bloody moths come from?"
  Thomas Eddison, 1879

- My American friend said his girlfriend had left him because he was 'un-American.'
  "Were you surprised?" I asked.
  "Nah," he said, "I could see it coming a kilometre away."

- I accidentally took the cat's tablets by mistake. Don't ask meow.

- I was admiring my naked body in the mirror when I got kicked out of IKEA

- My wife is threatening to leave me for never putting the toilet seat down. Honestly, I'm getting a little tired of carrying it around anyway.

- Robinsons and Wimbledon have just ended their 86- year association. A spokesman said, "The split was cordial."

- It's not time that puts the weight on; it's not the minutes; it's the seconds.

- What does a Jedis broken roof do? Leak Skywater.

- I went to the pub and said to the landlord; "I'm here to drink my troubles away." "What will you have?"
Me; "Water. I have kidney stones."

- Did you know that the only palindromic act (ABBA) had a palindromic hit (SOS) in a palindromic music category (pop).

- Dentist; "When was the last time you flossed?"
  Me; "You should know, you were there!"

- Just put £40 worth of fuel in the car. Cost me £75

- Gaining weight is a piece of cake.

- I get really mad when I can't charge my phone. My shrink says that I should look for an outlet.

- The dyslexic Yorkshireman who wore a catflap on his head

- I got fired from the glue factory. I told them where to stick it.

- People who post music puns should be band.

- It isn't a real party unless some drunken idiot makes a fool of himself by walking face first into a closed glass sliding door.

    I'm fine by the way.

- My wife just called me pretentious.

    I was so surprised my monocle fell out.

- My yoga instructor was drunk today. Put me in a very awkward position

- What drug killed the dinosaurs?

    A steroid.

- Two slices of bread got married. Everything was going great until someone decided to toast the bride and groom.

- Supermarkets are trialling dental services from next month. There will be an express lane for customers with twelve teeth or less.

- Just been to the doctor because when I open my eyes, I start vomiting. He said it was see sickness.

- I went to a Comedy and philosophy convention. I laughed more than I thought.

- What's the difference between a camera and a foot? A camera has photos while a foot has five toes

- If you're not supposed to drink WD40, why does it come with a straw?

- I got angry and threw my keyboard at the wall. That's when the shift hit the fan.

- I yelled 'Cow!' To a woman riding her bike. She turned and put two fingers up to me and ran into a cow. I tried.

- I married my wife for her looks. Just not the ones she's been giving me lately.

- An anteater walks into a bar, and the bartender asks, "Can I get you a drink"
  "Noooooooooooooooooooooo!"
  "How about something to eat"

"Noooooooooooooooooooooo!"
"What about some peanuts?"
"Noooooooooooooooooooooo!"
Frustrated, the bartender cries, What's with the long no's?"

- Son: "I've just watched a man do 50 press ups. Can you do that, Dad?"

  Dad: "I'm pretty sure that I could watch someone do 100 press ups, son."

- Just seen an Asian Elvis Presley impersonator. Amal Shookup.

- The computer hackers got away from the scene of the crime because they ransomware.

- My wife just said, "Is it me, or is the cat getting fat?"

Apparently, "it's just you." is the wrong answer.

- I've been asked to play the part of Brutus in the play Julius Caesar at the local theatre. I think I might have a stab at it.

- I stole a chicken today and had to make a run for it.

- It's not procrastinating if I have no intention of doing it.

- It hurts me to say this, but... I have a sore throat.

- Anyone want my old copies of Chiropractor Monthly? I have got loads of back issues.

- My wife told me to stop pretending to be butter.

Me; "But I'm on a roll!"

- I said to my wife; "These new scales are great. I can tell how much my poo weighs."

  Wife: "So you weigh yourself before and after and the difference is the weight of your poo?"

  Me; "Er, yeah, I guess you could do it that way."

- Wife: "Why did you buy a boat?"

  Me; "There was a sail."

- I said to my friend;" I've got a job at the bowling alley. "

  "Ten pin?" He said.

  "No, permanent. " I replied.

- I went to see the doctor about my blocked ear. "Which ear is it?" The doctor asked.

    "2022." I said.

- I've just found out that cock fighting is done by chickens.

    12 months of training wasted.

- There's no 'I' in denial.

- I don't like the word 'xenophobia'. It sounds so foreign.

- My friend called to say that an evil wizard had turned him into a tiny harp. I drove over to see him, only to find out he was a big lyre.

- Just joined an arsonists' dating site. I've already got 1200 matches.

- My kids refused to eat leftover pizzas, so my wife told me to throw them out, which I did. I still don't know what to do with the pizzas.

- Another 'world's oldest man ' has just died. This is beginning to look suspicious

- At the airport I overheard two guys saying they wouldn't like to be onboard a plane flown by a female pilot. How sexist! It's not as if she has to reverse the bloody thing.

- Today was the pirate's son's fourth birthday party. He didn't recognize him at first. He'd never seen him be four.

- My date tonight is over six feet six! I can't wait two metre.

- I shortened the rope on the bucket used to collect the village's water. Didn't go down well

- Vin Diesel only eats two meals a day. Breakfast and breakfurious.

- It's better to have loved a short person, than to have never loved a tall.

- I saw the Dalai Lama in the bookies. I guess he likes Tibet.

- Girls: just remember that it doesn't matter how much chocolate you eat; your earrings will still fit.

- Did you know that the platypus is one of the few animals which lays eggs and produces milk? This means it can make its own custard

- Yesterday, I went to visit the World's smallest wind turbine exhibition.

    Not a big fan.

- My girlfriend, who works behind a bar, broke up with me. I keep asking her for another shot.

- My brother got a Star wars tattoo on his cheek. You should see the Luke on his face.

- No one will listen to Whitesnake with me, so here I go again, on my own.

- I love it when people think that they are punishing me by not speaking to me.

- At the interview, they said; "Describe yourself in 3 words?"

Me; "Lazy."

- Someone called me 'pretty' the other day. Admittedly it was in the sentence 'you can be pretty annoying' but take them whilst you can.

- I got pulled over today, and the policeman asked if I knew why he pulled me over... I replied, ""Is it because you want to see how tall I am?""

    He said, ""Step out of the car, sir."" See, I knew it...

- I saw a sign today that made me piss myself.

    Toilet closed.

- Try my wife's cooking. You'll never get better.

- A big cat has escaped from London Zoo. Police have warned men, in particular, to keep away from it since it is partial to biting off men's penises. A spokesman said, "It's a tool eater jaguar."

- When I found out my toaster wasn't waterproof... I was shocked

- Everyone makes mistakes; expect me.

- Aliens. " Take me to your leader. "

  Me; "No, you'll only laugh. "

- 2,000 mockingbirds are also known as 2 kilo mockingbirds.

- I'm selling my racing geese. Let me know if you want a quick gander

- As soon as I was told to put on the hospital gown, I knew the end was in sight.

- I asked Frankie Valli what Spanish word for grey was.

    He said gris is the word.

- Wife came home with a ladder in her tights. What an amazing shoplifter

- The couple who put their bins out first are on holiday. There are green bins, blue bins and even a brown bin out. It's carnage!

- I swallowed an ice cube whole a couple of days ago and still haven't pooped it out. Getting worried.

- I introduced my toddler to my new neighbour. "This is Che." I said.

  "What's Che short for?" She asked.

  "Because he's two." I spoke.

- I wish I had never taught my ewe how to navigate a yacht. Now, that sheep has sailed.

- A naked man ran into the church, chased by police. They finally caught him by the organ.

- Had an interview for a camouflage expert job last week but I didn't turn up. Just called me to say I got the job.

- One thing about hairdressers; you have to take your hat off to them.

- Someone just asked me to sing a line from 'Don't go breaking my heart.'

  I couldn't if I tried.

- Just like sweets, music is better without the rapper.

- What does oblivious mean? I have no idea.

- Before I got married, I never realised that there was a wrong way to put milk in the fridge.

- I went to the doctors with a suspicious looking mole. He said they all look like that, and I should take it back to the garden.

- I spoke with a retired perfume maker, but I couldn't understand him. He no longer made scents.

- My sailor friend has a hat phobia. He is afraid of cap sizes.

- Customs officers have destroyed 1,000 kg of illegally imported Chinese dumplings. A spokesman said it was wonton destruction.

- Growing up, we didn't have a lot of money. I had to use a hand-me-down calculator with no multiplication symbol on it. Times were hard.

- Sometimes, you meet someone for the first time and realise that you want to spend the rest of your life without them.

- Girl: "Tell me something you've never told anyone else?"

  Me (whispering) " I think the owl people already live among us. "

  Girl: "Who?"

  Me: " Holy crap!"

- All odd numbers have the letter 'e' in them. You're welcome.

- I saw a chameleon today. I can only assume that it wasn't a very good one.

- I've been on so many blind dates, that I should get a free dog.

- My friend's wife fell over a few days ago and gashed her forehead. I called him last night and said, "How's your wife's head?"

"I've had better. " he said.

- I'm trying to sing a song about black sheep, but I can only remember my first two baas.

- Lucy in the Sky with diamonds.

   John Lennon was rubbish at Cluedo

- Somebody recommended that I put a bet on a horse called Landfill.

   It was a rubbish tip.

- My friend is a locksmith and a part time musician. He's just written a song which has a lovely key change.

- All my Father Ted DVDs have been stolen. Police say they have nothing to go on and on and on and on

- I was making a cup of tea for my wife and called to her; "Do you want a KitKat chunky?"

  I don't remember much after that.

- How long should someone help a neighbour chop wood for? Axing for a friend.

- I said to the doctor ""I'm having trouble pronouncing words beginning with F and TH," the doctor replied "well, you can't say fairer than that"

- Me, looking at a barn full of feed. "What's all that for?"

  Farmer: "The cattle eat it. "

  Me; "How big is the cat?"

- The Beastie Boys are releasing a 5-part anthology. Parts A-D are free, but you have to fight for your right to Part E

- My left a lovely note for me:

  'Hi sweetie, I've prepared dinner, it's already in the oven. You just have to light it; I've already left the gas on for you. Love you xxx'

- Jose Mourinho got an electricity bill from Manchester United for £17,000. He called them and asked how come he had any responsibility for it. " you went into the trophy room in 2017 and left the light on."

- I've started recording Britain's Got Talent, so I can block out all the acts and just watch the adverts

- The devil whispered into my ear; "You are not strong enough to withstand the storm."

  I whispered into the devil's ear; "I love your eggs."

- I said to my son, "I need a battery so I can tell the time."

  He asked, "Is it for a clock?"

  I answered, "I don't know! That's why I need the battery!"

- The bloke next to me was shouting really loudly 'Snowy', calling his dog. I now have TinTinitus

- Ja Ja Binks has a brother, who is a famous author. Jor Jor Well.

- I accidentally solved a detective case. I'm Sheer Luck Holmes.

- A woman gets on a bus with her baby. The driver says, "That's the ugliest baby I've ever seen."

  The woman sits down, fuming. She says to the man next to her, "The driver just insulted me."

  The man says, "You go up there and tell him off. Go on, I'll hold your monkey for you."

- Does the arachnophobia support group have a website?

- Interviewer; "So tell me about yourself. "

  Me; "I'd rather not, I need this job."

- Took my pet sheep for a walk and turned around at the end of the road. A policeman saw me and gave me a ticket for doing a ewe turn.

- According to a recent pole I took, everyone in the tent is angry.

- Doctor: " How often do you exercise?"

    Me; "Three times. "

    Doctor; " A day, a week, a month?"

    Me; "I have given my answer."

- There are some real weirdos on the internet. Someone messaged me to meet up in the woods for a naked satanic ritual and they never showed up!

- Apparently, neutrinos have mass.

    I didn't even know that they were catholic.

- My niece is training to be a hairdresser. I asked her if she'd ever given a henna rinse. "No, " she said, " but I once gave a duck a bath."

- Off to midnight mass. Anyone know what time it's on?

- My wife said she was fed up with me putting the name of a vegetable in every sentence.

    "Are you going to stop?" She said.

    "Not neccecelery." I said.

- If I put a copy of Macbeth on a dictionary, is it a play on words?

- I once won a lifetime's supply of spam, but I frittered it away.

- My wife rang me to say she had been stung by a wasp whilst playing golf.

  "Where did you get stung?" I asked.

  "Between the first and second hole." She said.

  " Better work on narrowing your stance a little."

- I found my grandfather's wig making machine in the attic. It's a family hair loom.

- I asked my wife what women really wanted.

  She said, 'attentive lovers'. Or ' a tent of lovers', or something. I wasn't really listening.

- I saw a tribute band, the Chickpeas, they couldn't play a Black-eyed peas song, but they could houmous one.

- My career as a gold prospector didn't pan out.

- I woke up with rice in my hair, ears and nose. Funny because I slept well and went to sleep as soon as my head hit the pilau.

- You can't laugh out loud in Hawaii, but you are allowed a low ha.

- My friend's wife revealed she used to be a hooker, on their wedding night.

    Played for Wigan, apparently.

- They don't make time machines like they are going to anymore.

- To be a successful fisherman, you have to be able to live on your net income.

- Don't buy the cabinet called 'commando' from IKEA.

  No drawers.

- Buckingham Palace was raided last night, and three royal, ornate chairs were stolen. They were later discovered in a greenhouse.

  A police spokesman said, "People in glass houses shouldn't store thrones."

- 4 men in a bar.

  1st one; "Let me buy you all a drink, it's my birthday, I'm George, after my patron saint,"

2nd: "Cheers, I'm Andrew, a Scotsman named after my saint."

3rd; "What a coincidence; I'm Welsh and named David."

4th man; "Unbelievable! I'm Irish and called Pancake."

- Deserts are dry. Arid it somewhere.

- I can only think of a few Motown groups. Three, maybe four tops.

- I've been learning escapology. I must get out more.

- My girlfriend sent me a text saying, 'Your great'.

    I texted back saying, "No, you're great."

She's so happy, but should I tell her that I was only correcting her grammar?

- Vampires aren't real, unless you Count Dracula.

- The delivery guy asked me the time. I said; "anytime between 8:30 and 5:30."

- I cycled to the shop today for a bottle of Scotch but was worried that I might get stopped and the bottle confiscated so I drank it at the shop. Good job I did, since I fell off 7 times on the way home

- Peruvian owls hunt in pairs. They're Inca hoots.
- Are parking spaces measured in parking meters?

- I can't stand people who contradict themselves. They're awesome.
- Just covered myself with a can of fly spray.
  Still can't fly.
- Old statisticians never die, they just get broken down by age and sex.

- People who enter staring competitions should take a long hard look at themselves in the mirror

- I'm a professional forger.
  I have the documents to prove it.
- I'm tried of dyslexia jokes.

- RNA jokes get lost in translation.

- The Chinese inventor of the telephoto lens has died.
  Tzu Minh.

- My fridge smells of basil.
  I think it's faulty.

- Two rabbits in the field eating lettuce.
  1st rabbit:" This lettuce tastes pithy."
  2nd rabbit:" That's because I just pithed on it."

- I surveyed 30 women about which shower gel they used.
  The overwhelming answer was, 'Get out of my shower!'

- I got promoted at my job at the crematorium.
  My boss said I'd urned it.

- Every time I think about Mickey Mouse I fall over.
  Think I'm having Disney spells.

- A crow walks into a bar.
  Barman says, "I hope your friends aren't coming later; last time there was a murder."
  .

- It's not time that puts the weight on; it's not the minutes; it's the seconds.

- Bought my wife a pug as a present.

Despite the squashed nose, bulging eyes and rolls of fat, the dog seems to like her

- Just passed a test which said I had an IQ of 175.
  Only 3 questions.
  Bank account number
  National insurance number
  A signed copy of my birth certificate

- A cute girl at work said she'd only go on a date with me on a day that doesn't end in 'Y'.
  I said, "Great! I'll pick you up tomorrow!"

- I told my girlfriend that she looks better without her glasses on.

She said that I looked better without her glasses on.

- People in Iran are terrified of spiders but in Iraq no phobia

- I saw two men wearing identical outfits and asked if they were a couple.

  They arrested me.

- My mate egged me on to sniff his sister's knickers.
  She was wearing them at the time which rather made the funeral a little awkward.

- Kids have been on eBay all day.

No takers, I might have to lower the price.

- The doctor told me I was going deaf. The news was hard for me to hear.

- Did you hear about the cockney who thought Anita Harris was a successful piles operation

- I've given up telling people that I'm not a quitter.

- My girlfriend broke up with me because I'm so handsome and too many other girls want me.

  She also said something about chronic lying disorder, but I wasn't really listening.

- The genie gave me one wish.
  I said, " I wish I could be you."
  "Weurd wush, but U grant your wush."

- Every 'C' in Pacific Ocean is pronounced differently.

- I pulled out a nose hair to see if it hurt.
  Judging by the reaction of the man asleep next to me on the bus, I'd say 'yes'.

- Not one to brag about the expensive places I've visited; but I've just got back from the vets.

- I was walking past a building site when the guy hammering, called me a "paranoid weirdo."

  In Morse code.

- Someone has broken into my house and stole all my fruit.

  I'm peachless.

- A bit of advice please.
  Is 'motherfucker' one word, or two? It's for a Valentine's card, so I want it to be right.

- I fought off an attempted robbery at my shop by using a labelling gun.

  Police are looking for a man with a price on his head.

- How does Darth Vader like his steaks?

  Well, done done done, done da done, done da done.

- I was going to get some pets but it's just a step backwards.

- "Hello?"
  "Hi, it's your Jamie's Art teacher here. Just calling to say he's a real Van Gogh."
  "Really? That's fantastic.."
  "Hold on, just calling to say the ambulance is here and his ear is on ice, but it's not looking great."

- 'Hello, Roman Tee Shirt Company? I ordered an extra-large tee shirt but you sent me 40.'

- If you can't stand music puns, you have my symphony.

- My son was doing his homework, and he asked me what I knew about Galileo.
  Me: "He's just a poor boy from a poor family."

- The best time to think about your retirement is before your boss does.

- Wanted: Someone to brush their teeth with me.

  Because 9/10 dentists say brushing alone won't prevent tooth decay.

  No weirdos.

- When my wife caught me standing on the bathroom scales, sucking in my stomach, she laughed, "Ha! That's not going to help!"

  "Sure, it does." I said. "It's the only way I can see the numbers."

- I don't advertise my lip-reading business.
  It's all word of mouth.

- Here's a small piece of advice.
  dvi

- The keypad on a calculator is not the most important part.

  It's what's inside that counts.

- I hate beggars, especially the way they rattle their cans to show how much more money they have than me.

- Just opened three birthday cards, and I've got £60 already!
  I love being a postman.

- I can now retire with £1,236,445 in my bank, after working hard all my life, scrimping and saving, and the bequest of £1,236,250 from my dead uncle.

- I left my job on the farm because they had no horses.
  I wanted something more stable.

- Jesus asked the man entering heaven why he was there.

"My son was born by a miraculous intervention from heaven.
He only ever told the truth."
Jesus was intrigued.
"Tell me, were you a carpenter?"
The man nodded.
Jesus- "Father?"
Man; "Pinocchio?"

- I knew instinctively that it would cost a lot to send my children to university.
My wife asked me how I knew.
"It's mostly intuition," I said.

- Is it wrong to drop off drunks at houses that aren't theirs?

- They say, 'never go shopping when you're hungry.'
  It's been a week now and I'm bloody starving.

- Have you heard about the blind Cyclops brothers?
  Neither have eye.

- If you are attracted to both men and women but they are not attracted to you; you are bi-yourself.

- Son: "Daddy, I'm going to be a socialist when I grow up."
  Dad; "Pick one son; you can't be both."

- I was having sex with my girlfriend, and she whispered- 'turn the light off and stick it my butt.'
  I probably should have waited for it to have cooled down first.

- If you work at MacDonald's and work a double shift, is that a MacDouble?

- Why are there Pop-Tarts but no Mum-Tarts?
  Because of the pastryarchy

- The doctor told me I had onomatopoeia.
  I said, "What's that?"
  He said, "It's exactly what it sounds like."

- How many mystery writers does it take to screw in a light bulb? Two. One to screw it in most of the way, and the other to give it a surprise twist at the end

- I found a £20 note today, and thought 'What would Jesus do?' So, I turned it into wine.

- When you try to prove to someone that something doesn't work, it will.

- 'Your opinion is important to us.' 'Please wait until it goes to voicemail.'

- What's six inches long, two inches wide and drives women crazy? Money.

- A boy was born who had Indian, Chinese, Irish and Italian grandmothers.
  They couldn't decide on a name for him.
  Then it hit them...
  They called him Ravi O'Lee.

- In my spare time, I help blind children.
  I mean the adjective, not the verb.

- What do you call an Instagram celebrity who got coronavirus?
  An influenzer

- Condoms don't guarantee safe sex anymore.
  A friend was wearing one when he was shot dead by the woman's husband.
- I was having dinner with my boss and his wife, and she said, "How many potatoes would you like?"
  I said "Ooh, I'll just have one please."
  She said, "It's OK, you don't have to be polite."
  "Alright," I said, "I'll just have one then, you stupid cow."

- I've always been against organ transplants, but then I had a change of heart.

- I struggle with Roman numerals until I get to 159.
  Then it just CLIX.

- Teacher said to me; "I bet you can't name two structures that hold water?"
  Me; "Well, dam."

- I was really embarrassed when my wife nearly caught me playing with my son's train set and I quickly threw a bedsheet over it.
  I think I managed to cover my tracks

- I was going to start a taxi business, but I found that I'd be driving customers away.

- The dentist said I had teeth like a sabre-toothed tiger- they were outstanding.

- The difference between a baby snake and an adult one is the baby snake has a rattle

- My brother's a butcher and he introduces his wife by saying "Meat Patty."

- 9 months pregnancy isn't really that long, it just feels like a maternity

- I stubbed my toe on a gold bar and shouted out Au, Au.

- I'm selling a beer called 'Responsibly'.
  Now you will be able to say you drink responsibly

- It's no wonder Cinderella was so poor at sports. Her coach was a pumpkin

- I was told that I have amnesia. I'm sure I'd remember something like that.

- what do you call a slow-moving poo?
  A turdle.

- My wife loves cats and so do I. The feline's mutual.

- The couple next door has done a sex tape.
  They don't know yet

- My Grandfather died because the report said he had Type-A blood.
  It was a Type-O.

- I only believe in 12.5% of the bible.
  I'm an eighth theist

- What has 2 butts and kills people?
  An assassin.

- If organ trafficking is illegal, what about piano trafficking?

- Feeling a bit down and my wife puts her hand on my shoulder and said 'Earth'.
  It meant the world to me.

- The overweight parrot sadly died but to the pirate, it was a weight off his shoulder.

- If Cinderella's' shoe fitted so perfectly, how come it fell off?
- A Frenchman walks into the library and asks for a book on warfare.
  Librarian: You'll only lose it."

- How do you send a lady hobbit into a deep sleep?
  Comatose.

- In my previous life, I was a flower I believe in reincarnation.

- You can get lawyers at IKEA now. They're cheap but you have to build your own case.

- Old gardeners never die, they just spade away.

- How do you know when you have run out of invisible ink?

- I had the sh*ts for 5 weeks. Good news is they're back to school next week.

- For Christmas this year, give your children a box with batteries in and a note saying; "toys not included." Follow me for more festive fun.

- Clones are people two.

- I had a discussion with my wife about how many lettuces to buy. We decided that two heads are better than one.

- Are workers at a match factory allowed to strike.

- The undertaker's wife had loose morals.
  Anybody cadaver.

- Just bought my wife something black and lacy.
  Hope the football boots are the right size.

- Me at a party.
  "What do you do in your spare time?"
  Her; "I stalk."
  Me; "Really? I like walks in the countryside and feeding ducks by the lake."
  Her; "I know."

- Forks have four prongs because if they had three, they would be called threeks.

- My aviary roof leaks when it rains.

It's getting on my tits.

- Just downloaded Encyclopaedia Britannica on audiobook. It speaks volumes

- You matter. Unless you multiply yourself by the speed of light squared. Then, you energy.

- The final exam in my weaving course is looming.

- My doctor complimented me on my choice of footwear.
  He said that I have serious healthy shoes.

- My business produces extra-large sinks. I'm going to give it a massive plug.

- If a Grizzly wears socks, it still has bear feet.

- When it's sunny, I go to the pub for a cold drink.
  When it's raining, I go to the pub to keep dry.
  When it's cold, I go to the pub to keep warm.
  I think I may have a problem with the weather.

- I've opened a shop in Jamaica selling glass oven-proof dishes.
  Pyrex of the Caribbean

- An unemployed jester is nobody's fool.

- Do people with a toe fetish ever get off on the wrong foot?

- My girlfriend said I didn't like her cooking, so to prove her wrong, I had another slice of gravy.

- I joined the Glen Campbell's fan club and now I keep getting cards and letters from people I don't even know.

- My wife remembers things that I haven't even done yet.

- I decided to take up fencing. Neighbour says I must put it back or he'll call the police.

- A big thank you (I don't think!) to everyone who said it's OK for pets to sleep on your bed.
  Now my goldfish is dead.

- I give generously to the local cat shelter. I'm a feline-thropist.

- I don't always go the extra mile, but when I do, it's because I missed my exit.

- My wife said that it doesn't look like I'm very good at shaving. Bloody cheek!

- My wife gave me a lovely surprise present of a wristwatch. I thought: 'Is this a wind-up?'

- Website: 'We use cookies to improve performance.'
  Me: 'Same.'

- My paper aeroplane won't fly. It's stationery.

- Man chopped down trees without reason. Locals are stumped.

- I thought I was supposed to get older and wiser, not older and wider.

- Got a raise today!
  It was my meds, but, hey.

- My wife thinks I'm a stud.
  She shot me with a nail gun.

- October and idiots are letting fireworks off! Way too early!, it's freaking the dogs out making them bolt and knocked over the Christmas tree!

- A light 4-seater aircraft has crashed onto a cemetery in Donegal. Rescue services have so recovered 236 bodies.

- Someone took the wind from my sails.
  I'm disgusted.

- Argentina has a surprisingly cold climate. It's bordering on Chile.

- It looks likely to be a cold winter. Squirrels are gathering nuts already. Yesterday my brother went missing.

- Why is no one ever the correct amount of whelmed?

- One way or another, I'm going to have to stop quoting Blondie lyrics

- My wife wants to know the secret ingredient for my recipe for chocolate cake, but me Nutella

- Took my wife out for a meal.
  She said she would pay.
  I said: "Don't be silly, just keep running. "

- I told the chimney sweep that I would sweep my chimney in future.
  He said; "Soot yourself. "

- Me; 'Alexa, remind me to go to the gym.'

Alexa: 'I have added gin to the shopping list.'
Me; 'Close enough.'

- Don't throw sodium chloride crystals at people. It's a salt.

- I've just crossed a homing pigeon with a crocodile.
  I guess that will come back to bite me.

- Let's get rid of democracy.
  All in favour, raise your hand.

- Once you've seen one shopping centre, you've seen a mall.

- Dog walkers?

Worst crisp flavour ever

- Someone asked me what the 9th letter of the alphabet was.
  It was a complete guess, but I was right

- The most important thing I learned in chemistry lessons was never lick the spoon.

- Bloody cat has scratched my Impressionist painting.
  It's a Clawed Monet.

- The bin man put an Alcoholics anonymous leaflet on my bin.

- I was unpopular at school, my nickname was 'batteries'.
  I was never included in anything.

- What colour do Smurfs go if you strangle them?

- Where are those sixteen chapels that Michelangelo painted?

- My Chinese flatmate said: "Have you seen my cocaine?"
  Me: "Yes, he was brilliant in The Italian Job."

- I have a fear of heights, but I don't shout it from the rooftops

- I was born to be rich. You can tell by how much money I spend.

- I told my wife that I was nipping out for some sewing thread.
  I actually went to the pub.
  Gone, but not for cotton.

- Carpenter ants are the same as ordinary ants, except rainy days and Mondays always get them down.

- What I lack in vocabulary, I make up for with, you know, stuff.

- Never trust a train.
  They have loco motives.

- My latest book is about a chef who goes vegan.
  Jack and the beans stock.

- What do we want!
  Hearing Aids!
  When do we want them?
  Hearing aids!

- When my wife died, I couldn't look at another woman for twenty years. Now, I'm out of prison though.

- I dreamt something bit me in the neck, but when I got up to check in the mirror, it wasn't working.

- The only thing a vegan kills is a conversation.

- Sooty and Sweep puppets, free to good home. Just want someone to take them off my hands.

- I didn't go to the Urology convention; I watched it on live stream.

- DNA says to another DNA,;" Do these genes make me look fat?"

- I saw a swordfish. Didn't know swords could fish, tbh.

- The next person who orders orange juice with pineapple and cranberry juice is going to get a punch

- I thought my girlfriend was the one until I looked in her wardrobe. There was a nurse's outfit, a French maid's outfit and a police uniform.
  I thought 'she clearly can't hold down a job.'

- I have a phobia about speed bumps, but I'm slowly getting over them.

- My Dad always used to say, "If you love someone, let them go."
  Great man, rubbish trapeze artist.

- My brother wants a job, so I suggested Search and Rescue- they're always looking for someone.

- I have a really stylish pair of trousers made from spider's silk. Only problem is that flies keep getting stuck.

- Does the letter 'W' start with a D?

- I called the police about a murder on my front lawn...
  But they said they couldn't do anything about crows and to stop calling them.

- Does anyone know the name of the river that flows through Stratford-upon Avon?
  Thanks.

- Does anyone know what the ship was called in Mutiny on the Bounty? Thanks.

- I went to buy my girlfriend a maternity bra.
  "What bust?" The assistant asked.
  "The condom. "

- I didn't enjoy my holiday at sea; the ship was full of male cats. It wasn't the Tom Cruise I was expecting.

- Fulfilled my wife's dream by getting married in a castle. She wasn't that impressed with all the bouncing around.

- Wife: "Do you remember what's the stupidest thing you ever said?"
  Me; "I do."

- Do not wrap Christmas presents when drunk.
  Btw, if you get a TV remote, I'll need it back.
  Thanks.

- I opened the door, naked, to the postman.
  He said, "How the hell did you get into my house?"

- Interviewer: "Where do you see yourself in five years?"
  Me; "My biggest strength is listening."

- My wife asked me to stop playing Oasis songs all the time.
I said, "Maybe."

- I dislike maths puns, but I will make one if I half two.

- The knight wearing a suit of pottery armour was Sir Ramic.

- My wife says she's leaving me because I'm a know it all.
I knew it!

- My American friend has opened a number of eye make-up shops in Austin, Houston, Dallas and Fort Worth.

It's his Texas Chain Store Mascara.

- When was young, Samuel Morse was considered to be dashing.

- My chickens have stopped producing eggs. I think it's the henopause.

- Just been to a rubbish cheese festival. There was only one cheese! It was the briefest.

- Helped my neighbour bury a roll of carpet in the woods last night. Her husband would have helped her, but he's out of town.

- I crashed the 4x4 whilst listening to Adele. I was rolling in the Jeep.

- I suspected my girlfriend was a ghost, the moment she walked through the door.

- The first five days after the weekend are the hardest.

- I hide from exercises: I'm on a fitness protection programme.

- My wife knows nothing about football, and I asked her if she liked George Best.
  "I prefer Zippy and Bungle." she said

- Anyone want to buy a broken barometer?
  No pressure.

- I always take my cow through the vineyard to my field. I herd it through the grapevine.

- The return of the Jedi is not possible without the receipt of the Jedi.

- I've invented a silicone implant which plays music! Now, women can't complain that men stare at their breasts without listening to them.

- My wife is fanatical about cutting out coupons. She's a cliptomaniac.

- Got an email from school inviting us to a 'Drugs and alcohol evening for parents.'
  A bit of a change from a Pie & pea supper.

- Boss; "I'm introducing random drug testing. "
  Me; "OK, but not crack."

- My book about radioactivity is getting glowing reviews.

- How many Freudians does it take to change a light boob?

- Two years ago, I started a support group for anti-social people.

We haven't met yet.

- If I was told to pick one word that describes myself, I'd pick 'Doesn't follow instructions.'

- Going to a murder/mystery night at the local bakery.
  It's a who doughnut.

- I always thought that I would mature like fine wine, instead it's more like milk: I'm getting sour and chunky.

- A policeman just stopped me and said he was looking for a man with one eye.
  I said he'd have a better chance if he used both eyes.

- I need professional help.
  A butler, cook and maid should do it.

- My brother is a kitchen installer.
  He's just been arrested for counter fitting.

- According to research, you will eat 23 spiders during your life. In reality, you can eat as many as you want. Go on, spoil yourself.

- My wife, Rosemary, is leaving me because of my obsession with pens. Bye Rose.

- I failed my English comprehension exam, but it was totally unfair- I'm going to start a partition.

- Me and my wife are fastidious. Well, I'm fast she's 'idious.

- Going to write a book about how to turn your basement into a spa, disco, games room.
It will be a best cellar.

- Just bought a MIG welder. Anyone know where I can get a Russian jet?

- My girlfriend loves to be covered in cheese. She's a cracker.

- Got attacked by the numbers 1,3,5,7,9.
  The odds were against me.

- A baby's cry is a beautiful thing. Unless it's 3 a.m. in the morning, you're alone and you don't have a baby.

- My son took his first steps this morning.
  The window cleaner is furious.

- My Roomba just beat me to an M&M on the floor. I think this is how the war between humans and machines will begin.

- Give a man mashed potato and he will eat for a day.
  Teach a man to do the mashed potato and he will win 60's dance-offs for the rest of his life.

- Little known fact:

Phil Oakey (Human League) had a sister who invented singing in pubs. Carrie.

- Spanish joke:
  "I told my Maria a funny joke and cheapest her pants."

- I lost my job shaving patients in preparation for spinal surgery.
  It was due to cutbacks.

- Doctors have discovered that wearing a baseball glove increases your chances of catching something.

- A Glaswegian brings his new girlfriend home to meet his parents.

  "This is Amanda." He says.

  Father; "It's a f*cking what!!"

- A jockey died today. His funeral is a week next Friday at 20/1.

- A T Rex and velociraptor were at the bar and the velociraptor points to a Triceratops and says, "Why does he always get served first?"

    T Rex says, "Because he was herbivorous."

- My new girlfriend said she was a big country fan, so I said, "China is huge."

- The doctor said, "Well, here's the good news- they're going to name a disease after you."

- I asked the librarian if he had the new book about small penises.

    "I don't think it's in." He spoke.

    "Yep, that's the one."

- I went for a walk with a beautiful girl this morning, then she noticed me and so we went for a run.

- There are two ways of arguing with a woman.
  Neither of them works.

- I said to Bill Withers.
  "Ain't no sunshine " is poor grammar.
  He said.
  "I know, I know, I know, I know, I know, I know, I know."

- My mate with a stutter was telling us about his Nana.
  In the end, we were all singing along to Hey Jude.

- What do you get if you cross a motorway with a fridge?
  Killed.

- Police have found a man's body in a crate of chickpeas.
  They suspect hummuscide.

- Do NOT read the next sentence.
  ooh, you little rebel.

- Is deduction the act of removing ducks?

- For sale, box of After Eights. Mint condition.

- Do Lynx helicopters smell nice?

- My grandmother is 80% Irish. Iris.

- I was in the pizza restaurant when a couple started arguing. I don't normally take sides, but they were distracted so I had his coleslaw and her fries.

- My wife said she was sick and tired of my childish games and was going to leave me.
  I said she couldn't.
  "Why not?" She asked.
  " Because Simon didn't say so."

- Dyslexics are teople poo.

- I always try to be the bigger person.

Cake helps.

- I know how to build a pyramid.
  Up to a point.

- Police have confirmed that the man who fell from the roof of the nightclub was not a bouncer.

- Never ask a woman drinking straight from the bottle, how's she doing?

- Bought a box of animal crackers but took it back because the seal was broken.

- You never know what I have up my sleeve.
  Today, it was a black sock.

- If you can make a woman laugh, you're almost there.
  If you're almost there and you make a woman laugh- different scenario.

- Do people offer Hank Marvin food every time he introduces himself?

- I was about to watch a documentary about the clitoris, but it was on the red button, and I couldn't find it.

- When I got the job at an Indian restaurant, I had to sign a naan disclosure agreement.

- I went to a fancy dress party as a screwdriver. I turned a few heads!

- Apparently, a home DNA test kit is not the best baby shower gift.

- Did you hear about the Peruvian baker who dropped a meat & onion pastry-based product on his foot? He's now on Inca Pastie benefit.

- I'm not saying it's rough where I live, but they were selling fake Primark clothes in the pub.

- Never odd or even spelt backwards is never odd or even.

- After four minutes into my run, I decided to work on my personality.

- I made a risotto with locally foraged mushrooms. It was delicious and accompanied by a flock of sheep singing 'Bat out of Hell' to an electric light show.

- I said to my hairdresser.
  "Give me a haircut like Tom Cruise. "
  He handed me a cushion to sit on.

- Went to the doctor yesterday. She said.
  "Have you been working out? You look trim; that colour shirt suits you."
  I think it was complimentary therapy.

- I complained to my GP about pains in my foot.
  He said, " Gout."
  Me; " I've only just got here!"

- I don't mind colouring books, but dot to dot is where I draw the line.

- What do you call a dentist who doesn't like tea?
  Denis.

- I took a bottle of tonic water to give the girl on our first date.
  Schwepped her off her feet

- I paid £30 for an online spelling course but didn't pass!
  I've been cheeted.

- I was setting the voice recognition password on my phone when a dog barked.
  Spent all morning looking for the dog so I can unlock my phone!

- Me;" I've taught my dog morse code!"
  Dog taps his paw.
  Wife: "What did he say?"
  Me; "woof."

- On average, a dog barks 25 times a day.
  That's a woof estimate.

- I've been learning how to estimate a dog's weight.
  Today, I picked up a few pointers.

- Does anyone know the name of the big bird on Sesame street?

- I bought a travelling iron yesterday.
  I woke up this morning and it had gone.

- It's been difficult learning to drive a golf buggy, but I finally got it down to a tee.

- Every time my doorbell rings, my dog hides in the corner.
  He's a Boxer

- Been blocked by Take That!
  Whatever I said, whatever I did, I didn't mean it.

- I've developed a rash on my upper leg, and every time I scratch it, I hear music.
  Doctor says it's spotty thigh.

- Boxer: 'Doctor, I have trouble sleeping.'
  Doctor; 'Try counting sheep.'
  Boxer: 'I do, but every time I get to nine, I stand up.'

- The Ministry for Unfinished Research has concluded that six out of ten people

- I've started taking my kayak out on the lake. It's exhilarating.
  I feel like canoe person.

- Someone has stolen all the bus stop signs around here.
  Where do these people get off?

- My job is making plastic Dracula's. There's two of us, so I make every second count

- My fridge smells of basil.
  I think it's faulty.

- My wife gets angry when she's given poor wine. If you add lemonade and fruit to it, she gets sangria.

- I was reading the dictionary in bed last night.
  I got up to P.

- I bought my girlfriend 4 pregnancy testing kits and they all tested positive!
  She started crying.
  "How can we afford 4 kids?"

- Dear autocorrect.
  "It's never 'duck'.

- I'm too easily distrac ·

- My back goes out more than I do.
  ·
- Hear about the Irishman who shot a gun at a wall and killed himself? Rick O'Shea.

- I tried some old Viagra, but they didn't work.
  Seems they were past their swell-by date.

- I went for a job in a sandwich shop, but they said the roll had already been filled.

- I went to the indoor climbing centre today, but someone had stolen all the grips!
  You couldn't make it up.

- I passed my paintballing exam with flying colours.

- I started a business selling bonsai trees.
  It was so successful that I had to move to smaller premises.

- My friend, Jim Apple, had a nightmare holiday in France every time he introduced himself.

- I see Billy Joel's laundry is still wet.
  He didn't start the dryer.

- Avoid being pestered by wasps at picnics.
  Smear your children with jam.

- I saw the ghost of a poodle/cocker spaniel cross.
  It was a cocker poodle boo

- My nickname at school was Scarface.
  I was really good at knitting.

- The first rule of Passive Aggressive Club is...
  ...you know what? Never mind. It's FINE

- Me, (nervously licking lips in anticipation)
  "I've never done a bungee jump before "
  Instructor: "Don't lick my lips again."

- I hate it when I wake up with a hangover, my eyebrows shaved off and a dick drawn on my forehead. Especially when I was in alone.

- If I had a penny for everyone who asked me to look after their dogs… I'd have a pound.

- I asked a priest if it was OK to kiss a nun.
  He said yes, as long as I don't get into the habit.

- I've just started a band called The Subtractions.
  Take it away boys...

- My window cleaner was cursing and swearing as he washed my windows with his sleeve.
  I think he's lost his rag.

- My wife asked me, "Are you sometimes surprised as to how little people change?"

I said, "Actually, the process is the same. Apart from their tiny clothes."

- Dorian Grey jokes never grow old.

- Helen Waite is in charge of our complaint department. If you want to complain, go to Helen Waite

- My hypnotherapist put an idea in my head to stop my drinking.
  It was a sobering thought

- I could hardly lift that bottle of water.
  It was an Evian.

- It's so hot, if Michael Barrymore invited me to a pool party, I'd probably go.

- Councils announce their delight at the hot weather as roads melt and fill in the potholes.

- It's the man who invented automatic tennis server's birthday today.

Many happy returns.

- I'm good at getting on aeroplanes.
  I went to boarding school.

- 5 years ago, our doctor was delivering Pizza and Coleslaw.
  My wife has never forgiven me for what I named the twins.

- I was once served French pancakes in a haunted house.
  They gave me the crepes.

- I took my granddad to one of those fish spas where fish nibble the dead skin from your feet.
  It was £50, but cheaper than a funeral.

- The trouble with counterfeiting banknotes is you can't make any real money

- A man walks into a hardware shop and says,

"One mousetrap, please and can you hurry?
I have to catch a bus."
" Sorry," says the sales assistant, "But our traps aren't that big."

- Growing up we didn't have a lot of money.
I had to use a hand-me-down calculator with no multiplication symbol on it.
Times were hard.

- A drunk walks into the library and says," burger and chips please."
Librarian leans forward and says, " this is a library "
"Sorry, " he whispered, " burger and chips please."

- I highly recommend the Adam Ant diet.
'Don't chew ever, don't chew ever...'

- Just fallen off a twenty-foot ladder. Good job I was only on the second rung.

- Discovered Pebbles in the pool filter.
  Fred and Wilma are devastated.

- Ever since I've been walking around wearing Hovis on my head, I've lost 10 pounds!
  It's a loaf hat diet.

- Ha- amusing
  Ha ha- funny
  Ha ha ha - sarcastic laughter
  Ha ha ha ha - staying alive

- Just killed a mouse with a baseball bat.
  Also banned from Disneyland.

- If you don't believe that I'm a singer in a Black-eyed Peas tribute band,
  Well I Am.

- How do you confuse a Scottish doctor?
  Tell him that you have 'knee problems '.

- Just bought a tin of molasses. Wonder what they do with the rest of the mole?

- One of my colleagues at work said to me: "Could you be any more annoying?"
  Tomorrow, I shall be wearing tap dancing shoes.

- The machine I bought for forging American coins doesn't work. I've tried the instruction book, but it just doesn't make any cents.

- Police are on the lookout for a man going around attacking people with knitting needles.
  They think that he's following a pattern.

- Despite cleaning all the stains off, I lost my job as a church window cleaner.

- I got to the final of the World's Most Congested Nose competition, but I blew it.

- I lost two fingers on my right hand and asked the doctor if I would be able to write again.
"Yes, but I wouldn't count on it."

- Getting fed up with people complaining about prices.
£2 for a coffee, £3 for a slice of cake, £5 for parking.
I'm going to stop inviting them around.

- Standing on the tube this morning I thought:" these pringles are going to be crushed."

- Did we ever find out what the knights in white sat in?

- Does an apple a day keep the doctor away, or is that one of Granny's myths?

- Enjoyable walk this morning with the dogs.
  I found an old grave headstone by the roadside and the chap was 114! He was Miles from London.

- I was just in the supermarket and man started emptying the contents of his trolley at me, first some custard, then jam, some fruit, whipped cream, a sponge cake, a bottle of sherry and finally some glace cherries.
  I warned him not to trifle with me!

- Alligators can live up to 100 years old. Which is why there is a good chance they will see you later.

- A ship carrying a cargo of yoyos has sunk; fifteen times.

- When the doctor said there was a cure for dyslexia, it was music to my arse.

- Facebook removed my joke about a rice cake. They said it was tasteless

- I told my friend that my aunt is in hospital and passing the time playing draughts, ludo, mah-jong etc.
  "Any chess?"
  "No, she's gone private."

- It's been 1 year, 12 days, 9 hours and 42 minutes since the doctor cured my OCD.

- The man who invented Tupperware has sadly passed away.
  The funeral was delayed by an hour because they couldn't find the correct sized lid for his coffin.

- Just had a bath in creosote.
  I thought I'd treat myself.

- Just been on a weekend residential course about reincarnation, very interesting.
  Mind you, it cost nearly £800, still, you only live once.

- I failed my ventriloquist's exam.
  Can't say I'm surprised

- Blimey; seems that all my family and friends have birthdays this year.

- The referee who introduced the red card has sadly passed away.
  His family and friends are going to give him a good send off.

- For sale; Harry Potter games- quid each.
- My favourite childhood memory is not paying bills.

- Saw Dr Hook in the 70s.
  Worst prostate exam ever.

- My wife is leaving me because of my obsession with TV police dramas.

For the benefit of the tape, she has just left the room.

- I've given up telling people that I'm not a quitter.

- Keeping tropical fish in your house can have a calming effect on your brain.
  It's due to the indoor fins.

- I'm getting stressed about taking Viagra.
  I'm worried stiff

- Just imagine the self-control needed to work in a bubble-wrap factory.

- I got drunk at the Opticians works party and made a spectacle of myself.

- I had a row with my boss at lunchtime.
  One of the perks of working at a boating lake.

- I asked for seconds at the local restaurant.
  Next thing you know, I've got two big blokes stuffing a wet sponge in my face and massaging my shoulders.

- I took my wife by the hands and looked her in the eye.

"I've something to say that will be really hard."
Nervously, she nodded; "go on."
"Ken Dodd's dad's dog's dead."

- I've just splashed out on a new toilet seat.

- I unexpectedly received an error message from my colour printer. It was totally out of the blue.

- Just built a robot frog.
  It's held together with ribbets.

- As I get older, I can sense women dressing me with their eyes.

- I'm almost a millionaire. I have all the zeros, just need the one.

- I think my girlfriend needs a new mobile phone. When I spoke to her last week she said, 'we're breaking up', my calls have all gone to voicemail since then.

- Doctor: "I have your results. "
  " Tell me then, I don't have all day."
  Doctor: "Who told you?"

- I had eczema, diarrhoea & haemorrhoids over the weekend... My best game of Scrabble ever!

- My Dad always said that it was rude to point.

Great Dad, rubbish bricklayer.

- All hotdogs look the same because they're in bread.

- Whoop whoop.
  Just won a year's supply of budgie seed.
  I'm absolutely trilled

- Really fed up with Amazon. Every time I order chicken pellets from them, I get an e-mail a few days later asking for their feed back.

- My target today was 8,000 steps. I popped into 'Spoons to use the toilet and did 12,000 steps.

- Sang some Billy Ocean songs at karaoke.
  I think the crowd liked me; they kept shouting:" You are soul!"

- I posed naked for a magazine today.
  The newsagent told me to get dressed but it was still £4.99

- I married my wife because I thought she was a millionaire.
  Turns out, she makes hats.

- Gutenberg:" I've invented the printing press!"
  Printing press: "You need to reorder cyan."

- Just rolled a joint.

Sounds cooler that I went over on my ankle.

- I put my phone under my pillow last night and this morning it had gone but there was a pound coin in its' place.
  Bloody Bluetooth fairy

- Spelling and grammar pedants should be ostrich sized

- I bought some HP sauce the other day. It's costing me 6p a month for the next two years

- My wife says I no longer do things to take her breath away.
  I've hidden her inhaler.

- My sex life is like a Ferrari. I haven't got one.

- My wife told me that I had to put a clean pair of socks on every day. By Friday, I couldn't put my shoes on.

- My mate said, "I bet I can guess who your favourite Glenn is".

   I said, "Go on then".

   He said, "It's either 'Campbell' or 'Miller'".

   Not even Close.

- My Great Grandma died after completing a Marathon, but hey, at least she had a good run.

- Accidentally used the dog's shampoo.
  I'm feeling like such a good boy.

- I'm in A & E because I swallowed a load of Lego the nurse said there's nothing to worry about, but I'm shitting bricks.

- What's four inches long, two inches wide, and drives women crazy?
  An empty toilet paper roll

- Just put a black hole in the lounge.
  It really pulls the room together.

- In the wife's bad books again...Got her some lorry oil for her birthday.

Apparently it should have been L'Oréal

- Unbelievable news out of Ireland: Cork man drowns.

- My dog only obeys commands in Spanish.
  He's Espanyol.

- I just made gold soup.
  Put 24 carrots in it.

- Teacher: "what's your favourite letter?"
  Student: " G, miss."
  Teacher; " why's that, Angus?"

- I think I have alcoholic constipation.

Can't pass pubs.

- I've just been arrested.
  I was in the car dying for a pee, so I did it in a coke can.
  The police stopped me and asked what was in the can.
  I'm now being done for possession of canapiss.

- I regret getting the tattoos of 15 different constellations on my face. I feel like I've been starred for life.

- My friend has an excellent nose for wine. It's shaped like a corkscrew

- I own a copy of Michael Jackson's Thriller without the other guy talking.
  It's Priceless.

- I've run out of toilet paper, so I started using newspaper.
  The Times are rough.

- My wife just asked me if her appendix scar made her look unattractive.
  Apparently the response of "don't worry love, your boobs cover it" wasn't the answer she was looking for.

- On Tuna tin's it says, "Dolphin Friendly" How do they know if they ever meet a Dolphin?

- Where do space pilots leave their space craft?
  At Parking Meteors.

- There's a lot of crap on TV.
  I'll have to put the budgie back in his cage.

- I am giving up Thanksgiving.
  I'm quitting cold turkey.

- Just landed in the UK after a long-haul flight.
  The crew were lovely, super, smashing, great.

It was a Bowen 747.

- My wife was telling me about an innuendo contest.
  So, I entered her

- I've only been on this cabbage and boiled egg diet for two days and I've already lost 3 friends.

- If anyone is spending Christmas alone this year, please let me know. I need to borrow some chairs

- What has four legs and one arm?
  A happy pit bull.

- My penis is the size of two Argos pens.

Also banned from Argos.

- Just been berated about my meat-eating by a vegan.
  I didn't expect the spinach inquisition.

- Completely misunderstood pride month.
  Anyone want to buy six lions?

- Robin: "The batmobile won't start."
  Batman: "Check the battery."
  Robin: "What's a tery?"

- A truck carrying incontinence pants has shed its load on the motorway. Police are warning of long delays due to rubberknickers.

- I joined a local club for people with poor eyesight.
  I'm glad I did, I bumped into a few friends that I hadn't seen for a long time

- I like ham.
  It would be a shame if you put an 's' in front and an 'e' at the end.

- On my walk this morning there were a lot of coins floating in the air.
  I thought, "looks like change in the weather."

- I phoned a friend this morning and said "I've split up with my girlfriend.

You wouldn't have a spare bed for a few days would you"
He said "yes actually I have"
I said "that's great thanks mate. She'll be round in half an hour."

- A search party sounds like a fun way to look for someone.

- If you take your age and add five, that's how old you'll be in 5 years' time.

- I got thrown out of Bird World yesterday for making a parrot laugh. It's polly tickle correctness gone mad.

- My new car has a switch that says, 'Rear wiper'.

No way am I pressing that!

- My cousin and I compete vigorously to see who can be more helpful. He just installed an elevator in his Mom's house. Dang. He has really upped the Auntie.

- Turns out that the bloke in the park was tying his shoelaces and didn't want to play leapfrog.
  My bad.

- The man who invented gravy granules has had the freedom of the city bistowed upon him

- How easy is it to count in binary?
  It's as easy as 01 10 11

And that's it for now, folks.

Laughter really is the best medicine.

Best wishes,

Robert.

@robertwlk

Printed in Great Britain
by Amazon